Mutiny on the School Ship Bounty

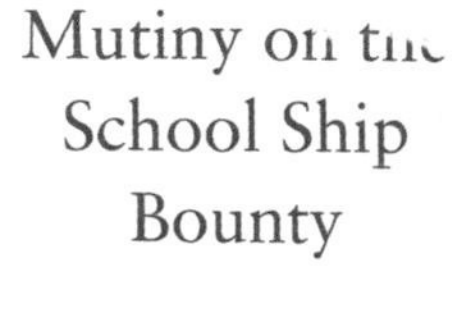

Mutiny on the School Ship Bounty

An Ayana Jones Adventure

Jon Blake

Illustrated by
David Roberts

Pont

First published in 2010 by Pont Books, an imprint of
Gomer Press, Llandysul, Ceredigion, SA44 4JL

ISBN 978 1 84851 038 8

A CIP record for this title is available from the British Library.

This book is published with the financial support of the
Welsh Books Council.

Printed and bound in Wales at
Gomer Press, Llandysul, Ceredigion

Purrlogue

Call me Purrpants. I'm a seven-year-old ginger tom. For the past five years I've been the school cat at the Owen Glyn Bowen Primary School in Abertwit. People don't see much of me, except at mealtimes, but I see everything of them. I whisper notes onto the dictaphone which I carry beneath my belly-fur, then type them up in the evening onto my PC ('pussonal computer', for those who don't understand these terms).

'A cat who can type?' you sneer. 'What kind of rubbish is this?'

'What?' I reply. 'Do you expect me to copy it all up in longhand?'

'But cats don't know human language!' you object.

'Think about it,' I reply. 'Cats have got all they wanted off humans for three thousand years. Are we going to blow it by admitting we understand what you're saying?'

Anyway, forget I told you that. It's

my job to open the door for you, offer you a comfy chair, and introduce you to a seafaring yarn called *Mutiny on the School Ship Bounty.* From time to time I'll be back to explain things, mend any holes in the plot, nudge you if you're falling asleep, and generally make sure your needs are catered for.

So, enjoy . . . unless you're reading this in a bookshop and haven't paid for it yet.

CHAPTER 1

AYANA JONES and Petal Starr stared into the great gaping hole with great gaping mouths.

'Yep,' said Ayana. 'That's definitely where school used to be.'

'Does anyone know why it disappeared?' asked Petal.

'People say it was built over an old coal mine,' replied Ayana.

'It could be Bad Karma,' suggested Petal. Petal's parents were rock stars and had taught her all kinds of twaddle that only rock stars believe in.

'I think I can see my rough book,' said Ayana.

'What does it look like?' asked Petal.

'Rough,' replied Ayana.

Petal stared hard into the void, trying to see what Ayana was seeing. Even after knowing her for two whole years, she still trusted in Ayana, because Ayana always seemed so *certain* about everything, whereas Petal's head was a frantic fishbowl of doubt. Sometimes

Petal would lie awake half the night, worrying whether it was right to eat a prawn, even if it was dead when she found it and had left a handwritten note specifically asking to be eaten. Ayana, on the other hand, only ever worried about not getting enough tea.

'Ah well,' said Ayana. 'I suppose we'd better be getting over to Uncle Bud's Burger Bar.'

Now that Owen Glyn Bowen Primary School had disappeared, Uncle Bud's was the only building of note in the seaside town of Abertwit, which was why Mrs Mostyn was holding assembly there. Mrs Mostyn was the head teacher of Owen Glyn Bowen, or at least the hole where Owen Glyn Bowen used to be. She was an absent-minded woman with a big fluffy halo of woolly grey hair round a big fluffy smiling face. In truth, she wasn't best suited to being a head teacher, or having any responsibility at all really, which was why she generally let Ayana make most of the decisions.

Such as where to have assembly.

'I think I might have a horror-muffin for breakfast,' suggested Ayana, as she and Petal wandered up the rickety high street towards Uncle Bud's.

'Sounds horrible,' replied Petal.

'Ten pence from every horror-burger,' announced Ayana, 'goes towards World Peace.'

'My mum says that's a racket,' replied Petal.

'Of course it's not a racket,' said Ayana. 'If it was a racket you could play tennis with it.'

'Eh?' said Petal.

'Cool,' chirped Ayana, glancing through the window of Uncle Bud's. 'We're last.'

The twenty-two other pupils of Owen Glyn Bowen Primary sat around three plastic-topped tables beneath a poster advertising Uncle Bud's Superjoy Meal Deals. Before them, on three grey metal stools, were perched Mrs Mostyn, Mr Woosnam and Miss Catsnap, the entire teaching staff of Owen Glyn Bowen. Mr Woosnam, who liked to think he was quite trendy but actually wasn't, sucked a Slurpy Creamsump through a straw. Miss Catsnap, who never wore anything other than a tracksuit and whistle, stared at the ceiling as if totally bored. Mrs Mostyn, who you already know, was making some ridiculous comment about imagining there was a mat like there used to be in Room 3 and everybody sitting in their usual positions, except Iolo Dorito who needed to be near the toilet door for reasons we won't go into.

'Good morning, Ayana and Petal,' said Mrs Mostyn, in that special teacher tone which means, 'Actually you're late.'

'Please, miss,' explained Ayana. 'We were looking down the hole.'

Mrs Mostyn gave her most disapproving look, which actually wasn't that disapproving. 'I did ask you not to do that,' she said.

'Yes, but only because it would upset us,' replied Ayana, 'and it didn't.'

'Nevertheless,' said Mrs Mostyn, 'a school rule is a school rule.'

'Even if there's no school?' asked Ayana.

Mrs Mostyn had no reply to this.

'Please, miss,' asked Petal. 'Are we going to have a new school?'

Mrs Mostyn smiled weakly. 'That is what I am to discuss with you this morning,' she said.

There was a dramatic pause, spoiled only by the final slurp of Mr Woosnam's Slurpy Creamsump.

'Owing to a slight oversight on my part,' continued Mrs Mostyn, 'the school was insured against fire, theft and dry rot, but not against collapse into a hole. Therefore there is no money to build a new school.'

'Bye then,' said Ayana.

'Hold your horses, Ayana!' rasped Miss Catsnap, without taking her eyes off the ceiling. Miss Catsnap had much more authority than Mrs Mostyn and could probably hold Ayana's horses herself, with one sharp blow on her whistle.

'I did not say there would be no school,' continued Mrs Mostyn, 'just that there is no money to build a new one.'

'You mean we've got to have an *old* building?' groaned Ayana. In Ayana's view, anything old was bad, and anything made more than a year ago was old.

'It is old,' admitted Mrs Mostyn. 'But it's not exactly a building.'

Twenty-three young brains wondered what Mrs Mostyn meant, while Petal Starr wondered about the word 'building', which seemed unbearably strange to her. It made sense to call something a 'building' while you were building it, but once it was finished, shouldn't it be a 'built'?

Petal often had thoughts like this. That was the reason she wore odd shoes and had her blouse tucked into her pants.

'If you all follow me,' announced Mrs Mostyn, 'I shall show you what I mean.'

CHAPTER 2

THE TWENTY-FOUR pupils of Owen Glyn Bowen Primary stood on the harbour wall and looked more puzzled than ever.

'But, miss,' complained Evan Biscuit, 'all I can see is chip shops, sweet shops, the yacht club and Mrs Morgan's seafood stall.'

'That's because you're looking the wrong way,' replied Mrs Mostyn.

'But the other way is out to sea,' complained little Evan.

'That is correct,' replied Mrs Mostyn.

As one, the twenty-four pupils turned and looked out onto the green-grey mass of water beyond the harbour. In the far distance a container ship was making its way along the coast. Closer to land, a few buoys bobbed about and the coastguard's rubber dinghy buzzed busily along. Apart from that, there was nothing except the rusting hulk of the SS Bounty, an old steam tramp which hadn't steamed for the past thirty years.

Worryingly, Mrs Mostyn's eyes were focussed on this very ship.

'Miss . . .' began Ayana. 'You don't mean that's our new school?'

Mrs Mostyn beamed. She could hardly contain herself. 'Now don't get too excited, children,' she warned. 'We can only use the SS Bounty if it passes its inspection.'

The children were not looking excited at

all. A few looked dumbfounded and most looked plain worried.

'But . . . it's a *wreck,*' moaned Shilpa Williams.

'It is a bit run down,' admitted Mrs Mostyn. 'But once we've got to work with some Brillo pads and poster paints, it'll soon look as good as new.'

'*We*?' repeated Ayana. 'You're saying *we* are repairing it?'

'Oh, Ayana!' trilled Mrs Mostyn, 'just think of the merit stickers you'll earn!'

Ayana was not impressed and neither were the other pupils. Mutterings and moanings spread the length of the harbour wall and were only silenced by a loud blast on Miss Catsnap's whistle.

'We start tomorrow, nine o' clock sharp!' barked Miss Catsnap.

'Yes, miss,' everyone sullenly grunted.

CHAPTER 3

IT WAS A lovely day as the pupils and teachers of Owen Glyn Bowen Primary set off across the bay in a creaky wooden dinghy. The sea was as still as a millpond and the sun shone like a great big yellow hot thing.

'Is it going to rain later, Mrs Mostyn?' asked Ayana.

'Not as far as I know, Ayana,' replied Mrs Mostyn.

'Then why have we got to wear wellies?' asked Ayana.

'That,' replied Mrs Mostyn, 'you will find out soon enough.'

Mrs Mostyn resumed her reassuring smile, a smile that Petal always found rather worrying. Mr Woosnam leafed lazily through his copy of *Ravemag,* and Miss Catsnap kept her hand steady on the tiller and her eyes fixed on the SS Bounty. They were approaching fast now, close enough to see the barnacles over the ship's bottom and the rusty rivets hanging out of the hull. Miss Catsnap steered the dinghy towards a ropey old rope ladder which hung down the side of the ship. As she pulled up alongside, a flock of birds rose and fled with unearthly cries.

'It's an omen,' said Petal.

'Nah,' replied Ayana. 'Seagull.'

Ayana was determined to be first up the ladder. Spurning all offers of help, she clambered up the swaying rope steps like a monkey, climbed over the guard-rails and dropped onto the deck with an almighty SPLUGG. To her surprise she had not landed on solid wood but into a kind of soft greyish mud which reached almost to the top of her wellies.

SPLUGG! Petal landed beside her.

'What is this stuff?' asked Ayana. She always expected Petal to know about nature because Petal's mum and dad saved rainforests and stuff, mainly by having champagne parties on their deluxe private yacht.

'I'm not totally sure,' replied Petal, 'but it looks like guano.'

'Guano?' repeated Ayana. 'Isn't that a type of fruit?'

'Not exactly,' replied Petal.

'How do you mean, "not exactly"?' asked Ayana, who always got frustrated with Petal's roundabout way of saying things.

'Well,' replied Petal. 'It may start as fruit, or it may start as fish. Then it goes through a gull's digestive system and comes out as guano.'

SPLUGG! SPLUGG! SPLUGG! A host of other pupils had unexpectedly soft landings on SS Bounty. Every one of them was in the guano up to their knees, except Roly Bogart, who had fallen into it completely. It was the kind of thing that happened to Roly all the time.

Mrs Mostyn took a register, then instructed Mr Woosnam to get the shovels. 'The first project today,' she announced, 'is to clear this lot overboard.'

Petal was aghast. 'But, miss!' she cried. 'We're supposed to think green!' Owen Glyn Bowen Primary had held an Environment Awareness week when Petal was in Year One, and she'd remembered every word.

'What are you suggesting, Petal?' asked Mrs Mostyn.

'We should put it in the sun, miss,' replied Petal, 'and when it's dry, cut it into squares and use it as fuel.'

'And where do you propose we do this?' asked Mrs Mostyn.

'The poop deck, miss?' suggested Ayana.

Mrs Mostyn sighed. 'I am impressed by your maritime knowledge, Ayana,' she said, 'but this ship does not have a poop deck. And besides, we do not need fuel, because we're not going anywhere.'

Ayana was gutted. 'Not going anywhere?' she moaned. 'But it's a ship!'

'It is a school ship,' corrected Mrs Mostyn.

'Exactly,' said Ayana. 'So we should have field trips every day, like going to different beaches and testing how warm the sand is.'

'This ship is owned by Abertwit Borough Council,' replied Mrs Mostyn. 'Abertwit Borough Council intends it to remain here, not in Pagwell-by-Sea.'

'But, miss!' groaned Ayana.

'Buts are for billy goats,' replied Mrs Mostyn, 'and if you lot don't get shovelling, there won't be a school at all!'

CHAPTER 4

IT WAS HARD work clearing up after the seagulls, but it did seem easier once Ayana got everyone singing a sea shanty. Ayana didn't know any real sea shanties, so she adapted *Sosban Fach,* with Mr Woosnam doing his human beat-box for accompaniment, except Mr Woosnam kept going out of time, sending all the shovels haywire and guano all over the shop.

Eventually, however, it was possible to see the deck again, and imagine what a fine ship the SS Bounty could be – once the galley, the mess, the cabins, the heads, the hold, the bridge and the engine room were clean as well. Still, that was nothing that twenty-four fit young people could not do, especially when divided into houses and put in competition for the school shield. Soon the sounds of scrubbing, sanding, scraping and out-of-time beat-box could be heard right across the bay, punctuated by an occasional shrill whistle as Miss Catsnap arrived in the dinghy with another consignment of desks, crayons and laminated factsheets.

Ayana and Petal were in charge of cleaning out the galley, which is what floating folk call a kitchen. They were amazed to discover that, among the old boxes and antique stoves, there was enough meat to provide for a week's school dinners. Unfortunately, however, this meat was still running round with long tails at one end and hideous yellow teeth at the other. Petal was not keen on eating it in any case, but Ayana insisted that there was a well-known dish called rat-a-too-ee which they could make once they'd brained the ugly beasts with a frying pan.

Mrs Mostyn was most pleased with the hard work the children were doing. She very much wanted to mark it, but as it wasn't done in an exercise book this presented problems. She tried chalking 'Well done, Chloe – a most original piece of cleaning' on the wall, but as Chloe then had to clean the wall again, Mrs Mostyn decided to leave things be and retire to the bridge. She sat back in her captain's chair, placed her feet on her captain's desk, admired the view, and pondered where to put her box of gold merit stars. For the first time since the school fell down the hole, she was starting to relax.

Mrs Mostyn's peace of mind did not last

long. Just as she had settled on a place for her stars, the door to the bridge flew open and in burst Ayana and Petal in a state of high excitement.

'Please, miss!' cried Ayana. 'Roly Bogart's crying!'

'Oh dear,' said Mrs Mostyn, wearily. 'What is it now? Nosebleed? Toothache? Pencil case gone missing?'

'Please, miss,' cried Petal, 'he opened a door and a skeleton fell on him.'

'A skeleton?' repeated Mrs Mostyn. 'A real skeleton?'

'Not a *total* skeleton,' said Ayana, reassuringly. 'It still had a bit of face on it.'

Mrs Mostyn went quite pale. 'I hope this is not one of your pranks, Ayana,' she said.

Unfortunately, for once, it wasn't. Roly Bogart was down in the hold, just as Ayana and Petal had described him, flat on his back with a skeleton pinning him to the floor. An audience of screaming children completed the picture.

CHARACTER NOTES by Purrpants

Roly Bogart is a total one-off. He looks like a cherub with baby-blonde curls, blue eyes, rosy cheeks and a squashed raspberry mouth. But on his skinny arm is a small tattoo of the Incredible Hulk. Roly, you see, does not want to be what nature has obviously cut him out to be - a meek, sweet little angel that all the girls want to mother. For this reason he speaks in a ridiculously gruff voice and hates to cry - though he does make exceptions, such as when pinned to the ground by a rotting corpse.

Mrs Mostyn was determined not be fazed by the situation. 'Can we have some volunteers to take the skeleton off Roly?' she enquired.

The screaming got a little louder.

'Who'd like to be skeleton monitor?' asked Mrs Mostyn, brightly.

The screaming did not stop.

'Fifteen merit stickers for moving the skeleton!' trilled Mrs Mostyn.

'Will you throw in a half-day holiday?' asked Ayana. She and Petal, unlike the other pupils, were not screaming. That was because Ayana and Petal spent half their waking hours watching horror films and were more used to seeing corpses covered in gore than normal living people.

'Um . . . I'm not sure if I'm allowed to do that . . .' murmured Mrs Mostyn.

'That's the deal,' replied Ayana. 'Take it or leave it.'

Mrs Mostyn ummed and ahhed, the pupils continued to scream, and Roly made a strange whimpery, gibbery noise which suggested he was keen on seeing his mum as soon as possible. As it was, however, it was Miss Catsnap who broke the deadlock, marching into the hold, casting Mrs Mostyn aside and wrenching the skeleton from Roly's prone form. The skeleton collapsed with a clatter into a bizarre seated position, revealing a few rotting rags of sailor's clothing and a wooden sign across its ribs.

The sign said 'MUTINEER'.

'You two,' snapped Miss Catsnap at the closest snivelling wrecks, 'pull yourselves together and take this boy to the medical room.'

'I've got some witch hazel in my first-aid box, Gretel,' said Mrs Mostyn, lamely.

Miss Catsnap gave a derisive sniff and led the two snivelling wrecks, and Roly, out of the hold.

Ayana's eyes fell on the sinister sign round the skeleton's neck. 'Please, miss,' she asked. 'What does "mutineer" mean?'

'Never mind that now, Ayana,' said Mrs Mostyn. 'Find a flag or something to wrap this poor fellow in so we can give him a proper sea burial.'

'Shouldn't we tell the police or something?' asked Petal.

Mrs Mostyn gave an awkward cough. 'This unfortunate wretch obviously died a long, long time ago,' she replied. 'Besides, we don't want police crawling over the boat when the inspectors arrive. That wouldn't look good at all.'

The unfortunate wretch was duly dispatched to Davy Jones's locker, clad in a makeshift sheet of out-of-date Owen Glyn Bowen tea-towels featuring the crudely drawn faces of long-gone pupils. Mrs Mostyn read 'The Owl and the Pussycat', which was the only poem about sailing in the school library, and Mr Woosnam played the 'Last Post' on the kazoo. But all Ayana could think about was the sign saying 'MUTINEER' and what this might mean.

When Ayana didn't get an answer to a question, she had a simple way of dealing with it. She repeated the question, and if it still didn't get a response, she repeated it again, and again, and again, for a day or more if necessary, till the other person gave in through sheer exhaustion.

Mrs Mostyn was not particularly difficult prey. She gave in by lunchtime.

'If you must know, Ayana,' she said, 'a mutineer is someone who takes part in a mutiny.'

'What's a mutiny, miss?' asked Ayana.

'Not something young people should get involved in,' replied Mrs Mostyn.

'Tell me more,' replied Ayana.

Mrs Mostyn was reluctant, but the thought

of another ninety questions from Ayana swayed her. 'A mutiny,' she proclaimed, 'is when the rabble rises up against the officers and takes over the ship.'

'Rabble, miss?' said Ayana. 'Is that like us?'

'Very like you,' replied Mrs Mostyn.

'Tidy,' said Ayana.

'I don't suppose the fellow we buried thinks it's tidy,' said Mrs Mostyn. 'He paid a heavy price for his rebellion.'

'Only because it failed,' replied Ayana.

CHAPTER 5

Little did Ayana know it, but a rebellion was already taking place on the SS Bounty. The skeleton incident had had a terrible effect on the other pupils, who had become quivering wrecks, unable to hold a paintbrush or flick a duster. Most of them had rung their mums and dads, and their mums and dads had decided they might be better off at another school. Even as Ayana was discussing the meaning of mutiny with Mrs Mostyn, Evan Biscuit's dad was on his way to the ship in his amphibious people-carrier.

By the time Mrs Mostyn realised what was up, it was too late. The pupils were on their way down the rope ladder and there was no way they were coming back. Even the promise of extra custard for school lunch fell on deaf ears. Ayana, Petal and the three teachers watched glumly as the people-carrier chuntered off towards the safety of dry land, where the only skeletons were safely stowed in the churchyard.

'That's it then,' sighed Mrs Mostyn. 'Two pupils. The game's up.'

'Not quite,' replied Miss Catsnap. Her laser eyes were focussed on the door to the purser's office, now the medical room, out of which the familiar figure of Roly Bogart was emerging, closely followed by the four helpers who had been detailed to look after him.

'What's going on?' asked Roly. 'Where is everyone?'

'Half-term holiday,' blurted Mrs Mostyn. 'For children with dark hair,' she quickly added.

Roly Bogart frowned and pursed his little raspberry mouth. 'Suki Pugh's got dark hair,' he pointed out, Suki Pugh being one of his helpers.

'Dark hair . . . and broken teeth,' blabbed Mrs Mostyn. She was a hopeless liar.

'I've got a broken tooth and dark hair,' piped up Iolo Dorito, another helper. 'Why aren't I on half-term holiday?'

Now Mrs Mostyn was really stumped. 'You are!' she trilled. 'Have a nice time.'

Iolo Dorito broke into a little jig of joy, but this was quickly halted by Miss Catsnap. 'You're going nowhere!' she barked.

Mrs Mostyn objected weakly, but Miss

Catsnap had had enough of the charade. She adopted her toughest feet-apart pose and addressed the confused pupils. 'This is the situation,' she said. 'The other children have abandoned ship. They did this because they are cowards and weaklings. You, however, are staying to finish the job we started and prepare the school for its inspection.'

There was a shocked silence, followed by a little sob, followed by a mumble of 'I want to go home'. Miss Catsnap's speech had not had the effect she was hoping for.

Ayana watched all this with increasing desperation. The longer she'd been on board SS Bounty, the more she'd grown to like life on the ocean wave. Going to school on a ship would be cooler than cool, especially when the alternative was Pagwell Primary, which had homework every night and a vomitous purple uniform.

There was only one thing for it. Ayana would have to inspire the others to stay. Ayana would have to make one of those speeches people make in Hollywood movies, the kind which win the day and turn the tide and change the course of history.

'Listen, you guys!' she cried. 'Don't let anyone take your dreams from you, because if you lose your dream . . . you don't have a dream anymore! We've got to believe in ourselves and follow our dreams because, if you believe in yourself and follow your dream, you can achieve anything!'

The sobbing and the moaning quietened.

Ayana moved in for the kill. 'Maybe the others are bigger than us!' she railed. 'Maybe they've got fancy cars and designer clothes and everything that money can buy! But we've got something that money can't buy! Something called . . . a dream!'

Roly Bogart's lip quivered, and he quickly wiped a tear from his eye. Now Ayana knew she had got them.

'Now go back to your work,' she cried, 'and make that dream come true!'

There was a cheer. As one, the other pupils marched back to their posts.

'Very good, Ayana,' trilled Mrs Mostyn. 'What did it mean, exactly?'

'You wouldn't understand,' replied Ayana.

CHARACTER NOTES by Purrpants

As you will have noticed, a number of new characters, about which you know nothing, have suddenly appeared in the story. These characters will not be going away, so pay attention carefully as I introduce them to you.

SUKI PUGH

Suki is a serious girl, spelt S.E.R.I.O.U.S. Suki does not do jokes, or trivial conversations, or anything that might cause the corners of her mouth to turn ever-so-slightly upwards. Suki reads serious books, watches serious TV programmes, and only plays one computer game – chess. People would probably give her a hard time about it, if she didn't have a junior black belt in Tae Kwon Do.

JESSICA TEW

Jessica Tew is a twittery thing, often difficult to understand as every sentence ends in a fit of sniggery giggles. Jessica is obsessed with the colour pink. Tough girls avoid her because she's so girly. Girly girls also avoid her because she's too girly even for them. But she does win every prize at the school Eisteddfod and plays piano to level 969.

ABDI BABB

Abdi Babb always has a cheerful smile and enthusiasm for everything. Unfortunately, however, he lives in a place called Planet Abdi which is totally different to Planet Earth. It is wise not to take anything he says at face value. For instance, Abdi has never been to space, or died and come back to life, or won an Olympic gold at weightlifting. Worryingly, however, Abdi really does believe these things are true.

IOLO DORITO

Iolo Dorito is a squat, greasy-haired, spotty individual, and if you don't

like the stuff that comes out of noses, you certainly won't like Iolo, because he has lots of it. Iolo's favourite hobby is moaning, although in a good mood he does tell jokes that no one understands.

I hope this helps with your understanding of our story, to which we will now return.

Never had the pupils of Owen Glyn Bowen Primary worked so hard. Inspired by Ayana's great speech, they tore into their tasks like demons, spiriting away the dust and dirt of ages, clearing and cleaning, painting and varnishing. Every now and again someone would begin to flag, at which point Ayana would leap to the rescue and make her speech again, adding new bits about miracle births and poor blind puppies that learned to see. Home time came and went, and still the pupils worked, till the sun set on the watery horizon and a sliver of milky moon lit their frenzied efforts.

It was just as well the SS Bounty was making fast progress. Mrs Mostyn had a dramatic announcement to make.

'The inspectors,' she informed everyone, 'are coming tomorrow.'

'Tomorrow?' replied Ayana. 'Isn't that a bit soon?'

'In my opinion,' said Mrs Mostyn, with a knowing tap on her nose, 'they do not want us to succeed.'

Ayana fumed. 'You see, everyone?' she railed. 'They want to destroy our dreams! Well, they've got another think coming, because by nine o'clock tomorrow morning, the SS Bounty will be a fully-fitted, spick-and-span, ready-for-action school, or my name's not Ayana St Vincent Jones!'

It was another inspiring speech, but by now it really was getting very late. Even the keenest pupils were getting tired, and Iolo Dorito was getting very tired. Being Iolo Dorito, he wanted everyone to know about it. As he moaned about his aches and pains, so the mood changed, and there was talk about the hopelessness of the pupils' task and the general unfairness of life.

At this point Mr Woosnam stepped into the fray. 'Listen, guys,' he said. 'I've got a cool idea. Why don't we create a chill-out space on the bridge so when you guys need a break, you can just put your feet up? I could get out my guitar and create a good vibe, maybe sing some old Dylan numbers, unless you'd prefer something more modern, like the Spice Girls.'

Mr Woosnam's speech may not have been as great as any of Ayana's speeches, but it had an equally electrifying effect. All the pupils went back to work without another word, and no further complaint was heard.

CHAPTER 6

DAWN HAD BROKEN over the yardarm before Ayana and the others had finished their work. The final job was to assemble the desks in the new classrooms, each under a different porthole, bring in the storage units, the whiteboards and the chairs, and, in one last desperate effort, paint everyone's face for a wall-frieze. That done, the pupils and teachers sat in their places, ready for morning school, and, almost as one, fell asleep.

There is no deeper sleep than the sleep after a good day's work, except, maybe, the sleep after a good day-and-night's work. Ayana and friends were as dead to the world as the old mutineer, undisturbed by the screeches of gulls, the plash of the waves, or the soft, sinister footsteps of the school inspectors.

In fact, Ayana would probably have slept all day, were it not for the bellowing voice of Captain Horatio Blight.

'*What* do you think you're doing, asleep in class?' he bellowed.

Ayana shot upright, as did every pupil on

board SS Bounty. They found themselves faced by a tower of a man, ramrod straight, dressed half in naval uniform, half in teacherly civvies. A mass of curling grey hair sprouted from his nose and ears, which made some amends for the complete lack of it on the top of his head. The man's mouth was a lipless slit, his nose a hooked beak, sharp enough to open a tin can; his chin was an upward curving monstrosity, anxious to make the acquaintance of the said nose. But it was the eyes which held you. The eyes were stormy-ocean grey, utterly firm in purpose, with more than a hint of bitter cruelty. They were not eyes you would want to come upon unexpectedly in the dead of night. Or, for that matter, around mid-morning break time.

'Please, sir,' said Petal, 'but who are you?'

Captain Horatio Blight wheeled like a gun turret to face a very nervous-looking Petal. 'For your information,' he boomed, 'I am the new captain of this vessel.'

'Where's Mrs Mostyn?' asked Ayana.

Captain Blight spun back round. His brow furrowed. Something about Ayana caused him instant displeasure.

'Where is Mrs Mostyn, *sir?*' he snapped.

'Isn't that what I just asked?' replied Ayana.

'I am your superior officer!' roared Captain Blight. 'You will address me accordingly! Miss Catsnap, take this pupil's name and put her on half rations till Tuesday.'

Miss Catsnap snapped into action, pencil and notebook at the ready. 'Name?' she barked.

'You know my name, miss,' replied a baffled Ayana.

'We're doing things by the book now,' snapped Miss Catsnap. 'Give me your full name, including surname and any peculiar middle names you'd rather people didn't know about.'

'You'll be given rank and registration number,' added Captain Blight.

Ayana decided it would be best to comply. At least then Captain Blight might answer her question.

'Mrs Mostyn has been dismissed,' Captain Blight duly informed the pupils.

A cry of alarm went round the class. 'Why, sir?' came a nervous murmur.

'Why?' barked Captain Blight. 'For allowing the crew to sleep on her watch! A capital crime on the high seas!'

'So are you . . . our new head?' asked Petal. 'Sir,' she quickly added.

'This, young lady, is a ship,' replied Captain Blight. 'She does not have a head: she has a captain. Miss Catsnap is now first mate, and Mr Woosnam has been demoted to caretaker and cook.'

It was the first time the pupils had noticed Mr Woosnam, who stood by the door in a tatty old dustcoat with a ring of keys in his hand. 'You can call me Steve now,' he beamed.

'Miss Catsnap!' rasped Captain Blight. 'Hand the pupils their homework diaries and their timetables.'

	06.00–09.00	09.00–12.00	12.00–13.00	13.00–15.00	15.00–18.00
MON	Drill	Recitation	Rations & punishments	Three Rs	Singing
TUES	Drill	Recitation	Rations & punishments	Three Rs	Prayers
WEDS	Drill	Recitation	Rations & punishments	Three Rs	Dictation
THURS	Drill	Recitation	Rations & punishments	Three Rs	Swabbing decks
FRI	Drill	Recitation	Rations & punishments	Three Rs	Knot making
SAT	Drill	Recitation	Rations & punishments	Three Rs	History of the glorious British Empire
SUN	Drill	Recitation	Rations & punishments	Three Rs	Award of certificates and dunce's caps

With growing dread, Ayana looked down at the timetable that Miss Catsnap slapped onto her desk.

It was not like any timetable Ayana had ever seen. Monday to Sunday? Wasn't that every day of the week, and no weekend? And as for the subjects, where were the art, the science, the games and all the fun things they used to do?

'Drill?' she asked. 'Are we learning to be dentists, sir?'

'You are not!' rasped Captain Blight. 'And neither are you learning to be comedians! Now get down on the deck, the lot of you, and give me ninety-nine press-ups!'

The press-ups were only the start of it. Captain Blight's idea of school made training for the SAS look like a picnic. As far as Captain Blight was concerned, all children were born full of sin and the only way to get shot of it was to work their brains and bodies to the limit. Except that Ayana had already reached her limit getting the ship ready, and by the time she'd done all her allotted tasks, she was so far past her limit, if she looked back, she couldn't even see it.

At last Captain Blight rang the bell which

signified the shift was changing. Dog-tired, Ayana sloped back to her cabin, but on the way came across Petal, who didn't look tired at all.

'I've just spent two hours polishing the bilge pump!' moaned Ayana. 'What have you been doing?'

'Macramé,' replied Petal.

'Macramé?' repeated Ayana. 'What's macramé?'

'Making things with string,' replied Petal.

'That's all you've done?' gasped Ayana. 'Make things with string?'

'Well, rope actually,' replied Petal.

Ayana was flabbergasted. 'What did you make?' she asked.

'A cat,' replied Petal.

'You made a cat out of rope?' scoffed Ayana.

'Miss Catsnap *said* it was a cat,' replied Petal, 'but it doesn't look like one to me.' She opened her school bag and unrolled her afternoon's work. 'It's got nine tails,' she said.

Ayana's mouth dropped as it became horribly clear what her best friend was holding. 'A cat-o'-nine-tails!' she gasped.

'Like I said,' replied Petal.

'Petal,' said Ayana. 'You've just made a lash!'

Petal looked at her macramé project with new eyes. 'What – like an eyelash?' she asked.

'Like a whiplash!' cried Ayana. 'For beating people!'

Petal's face fell.

'People like us!' added Ayana.

Petal's face fell further. 'I've got to take it to the Captain,' she murmured.

'Throw it overboard!' demanded Ayana.

Petal froze, unsure what to do next. Ayana had no such problem. She seized the cat-o'-nine-tails and marched towards the edge of the ship – straight into the grim stone statue that was Miss Catsnap.

'I'll take that, thank you, Ayana,' she snapped.

CHAPTER 7

THAT WAS THE last straw for Ayana. It was bad enough having to do Drill and Recitation and hours of hard labour, but getting the lash instead of losing a merit sticker . . . that really did suck. As soon as the coast was clear, she gathered together everyone on her watch.

NOTE FROM PURRPANTS

If you check out 'watch' in a dictionary, you'll realise that Ayana did not have six people standing on her wrist.

'We've got to do something,' declared Ayana. 'Captain Blight's got a cat-o'-nine-tails and he's going to use it!'

'That's ridiculous,' replied Suki. 'Corporal punishment in schools was banned in 1986.'

'On land, maybe!' said Ayana. 'This is the high seas!'

'What do you suggest, Ayana?' asked Mr Woosnam.

'It's obvious,' replied Ayana. 'We've got to get rid of him.'

'Get rid of him?' repeated Jessica. 'How do you propose to do that?'

'Brain him with an anchor,' suggested Ayana.

Jessica paled. Ayana was always suggesting dangerous things, usually the first things that came into her head, and never seemed to realise how dangerous these things were.

'That would be encouraging violence, Ayana,' Mr Woosnam pointed out.

'It would be very encouraging violence,' said Ayana.

'We should try appealing to his better side,' suggested Mr Woosnam.

'What if he hasn't got one?' asked Ayana.

'Then we brain him with an anchor!' said Abdi, the only person who never seemed to worry about Ayana's mad ideas.

'How are we going to get the anchor up?' asked Suki. 'It weighs a ton.'

'Use something else then,' said Ayana.

'Like what?' grumbled Iolo.

'I know!' said Abdi. 'Remember that story, where the woman kills her husband with a frozen leg of lamb?'

'There's no lamb in the freezer,' replied Suki.

'What is there?' asked Ayana.

'Pizza,' replied Petal.

'Thin 'n' crispy?' asked Ayana. 'Or deep pan?'

'Does it matter?' asked Petal.

'Of course it matters!' snapped Ayana. 'We'll never brain him with a thin 'n' crispy!'

'No one's in the galley,' said Suki. 'Let's go and check.'

The nervous gang of would-be rebels made their way to the cramped little galley, where a tired generator rumbled and grumbled in the corner, spewing out just enough electricity to keep an old chest freezer chilly. Ayana and Suki rooted through the packs of frozen veg, while Petal's eyes were drawn to a trapdoor in the galley ceiling. 'I wonder where that door goes?' she asked.

'That's typical of you, Petal,' huffed Ayana. 'We're all concentrating on braining the Captain, and you're going on about a door in the ceiling!'

'It must be there for something,' mused Petal.

'Found the pizzas!' announced Suki, brandishing a box that must have been half a metre wide.

'What does it say?' asked Ayana.

'Stone baked . . . three cheese topping . . . special offer . . . use by 12 Feb . . .'

'It's past its use-by date,' warbled Jessica.

'Oh, right!' sneered Abdi. 'We can't hit him with it then!'

'Just tell us if it's deep pan!' snapped Ayana.

'Doesn't say,' replied Suki. 'But it feels quite heavy.'

'Give it here,' said Ayana. She took the pizza and weighed it up in her hand. 'That'll do the job,' she said. 'Let's go.'

'Wait,' said Mr Woosnam. 'We still haven't tried appealing to his better side.'

'OK,' said Ayana. 'I'll try appealing to his better side, and if doesn't work . . . the mutiny begins.'

It was the first time anyone had used the word 'mutiny', and there was an audible gasp.

'It's not a r-real mutiny though,' peeped Jessica, 'because then we'd be mutineers.'

Everybody remembered the sign round the skeleton's neck.

'Jessica,' said Ayana. 'We're going to kill the Captain and take over the ship. What would *you* like to call it?'

'Kill him?' said Suki. 'I thought you were just going to knock him out.'

'Did I say that?' said Ayana.

'I do think we should just knock him out, Ayana,' suggested Mr Woosnam.

'Then what are we going to do with him?' asked Ayana.

'There's a rubber dinghy in the hold,' said Suki. 'We could set him adrift in that.'

Ayana looked disappointed. 'OK,' she grumbled. 'We'll do that.'

'It's still not a mutiny,' whimpered Jessica.

'Don't worry, Jessica,' replied Mr Woosnam. 'Ayana is going to appeal to Captain Blight's better side first, and I am confident he will realise he has been rather too harsh, and change his attitude, and not only make this a friendly, happy ship but also begin to work towards world peace.'

'Whatever,' said Ayana, testing the mettle of the frozen pizza against the oven door.

The sea swelled ominously and the night lurked crow-black as Ayana knocked on the door to the bridge.

'Who's there?' said a gruff voice.

'It's Ayana, Captain,' replied Ayana. 'I've brought you a cup of tea.'

'Did I order a cup of tea?' barked Captain Blight.

'No, sir,' replied Ayana. 'I was using initiative, sir.'

There was a moment's silence.

'Bring it in,' growled the Captain.

Ayana entered the bridge. Captain Blight stood alone, faintly heroic in his greatcoat and cap. Even though the ship was still at anchor, his hands were fixed on the wheel, his eyes were fixed on the dials, and Ayana did not even warrant a glance.

'Leave it on the table,' he ordered.

Ayana did so. Time passed, during which it gradually became clear to Captain Blight that Ayana had no intention of leaving. He turned his hooked face towards her with an unwelcoming scowl.

'Any further business?' he barked.

'Do you take sugar?' asked Ayana. 'I haven't put any in, but I've got three lumps in my pocket.'

'No,' replied the Captain, with fearful resolve. 'I do not take sugar.'

'Are you sweet enough, sir?' asked Ayana.

The Captain's brow furrowed. 'I beg your pardon?' he growled.

'Are you sweet enough, sir?' repeated Ayana. 'It's what people say.'

The Captain's face set as grim as granite. 'Not to me,' he growled.

By now it was clear to Ayana that Captain Blight's better side had abandoned ship many moons ago. But she had promised to do her best to find it, so pressed on.

'Have you captained many ships, Captain?' asked Ayana.

Captain Blight's eyes narrowed. 'Have you no work to be doing?' he growled.

'I'm off duty, sir,' replied Ayana. 'And I was only asking, sir, because I was thinking of doing a project about you.'

Captain Blight turned his full attention on Ayana. He did not seem impressed by what he saw. 'You'd better get the record right,' he declared. 'I've captained a score and five vessels.'

'A score and five,' repeated Ayana, as if making a mental note. 'And were they all school ships?'

'Not at all,' barked the Captain. 'Whalers, every one of them.'

'Whalers?' repeated Ayana. 'What, like whale-watching ships?'

Captain Blight's brow knitted as hard as anchor-chain. 'Whale *watching*?' he scoffed. 'What would I want to *watch* a whale for?

The whale was put on earth to give us meat and oil, buggy whips and carriage springs, corset stays and fishing rods! But try telling that to the do-gooders with their stupid, sentimental ideas and godforsaken whale-song records!'

A small brim of froth had appeared at the Captain's mouth.

'Thank you, sir,' said Ayana. 'I've got enough information for my project now.'

It was if nature knew what was in store. The sea heaved and frothed and the rain lashed remorselessly as Ayana tottered from side to side back towards the galley. There was not a soul in sight, exactly as the rebels had planned. It was better for everyone to keep a low profile till the business was done.

Opening the door to the galley, however, Ayana was surprised to find Petal, still standing in the same position as twenty minutes earlier, staring at the ceiling.

'Petal!' whispered Ayana. 'You're supposed to be in your quarters!'

'It must be there for a reason,' muttered Petal.

'Forget the trapdoor!' hissed Ayana. 'We've got more important things to think about!'

Ayana's furtive fingers scrabbled through the freezer cabinet and emerged with the pizza they'd found earlier. She removed the cardboard box and tested it again against the side of the galley.

'Are you going to do it?' asked Petal, half-enthralled, half-terrified.

Ayana nodded. 'Wish me luck, Petal,' she said, grasping her hand in their special secret handshake.

'Be careful,' said Petal.

'Here goes nothing!' replied Ayana.

Ayana returned to the deck, clutching hard onto her frozen pizza as the wind tore and the rain lashed. With grim determination she made her way up the slippery steps towards the bridge, and, arriving at the door, began to summon up the spirit of her ancestors. This was something Ayana did when she needed strength, but not often, as Ayana's ancestors came from just about everywhere on earth, and summoning them up took ages.

When the strength was within her, Ayana oh-so-slowly lowered the door handle, and slipped inside, as silent as silk. Captain Blight remained exactly as before, facing out to the cruel sea, memories of a thousand whale chases beating around his weather-beaten brow.

With the sure, silent feet of a jungle cat, Ayana crept up behind him.

For a brief moment Captain Blight seemed to catch wind of something. He cocked his head very slightly to one side. Then he was lost once more in his memories.

Soon, thought Ayana, he would be lost in dreams instead.

Ayana took hold of the pizza with both hands and raised it high. Dimly, she realised just how tall Captain Blight was . . . but she was already committed to the strike.

THUNK!

What a blow Ayana delivered. Such a shame it landed halfway up the Captain's back, the highest point Ayana could reach without standing on a chair. The Captain staggered forward a little, gave a grunt of surprise but, other than that, seemed miraculously unharmed.

Whether Ayana could now stay unharmed was another question. Suddenly she found herself face to face with the mighty Blight, whose face first registered bafflement and then fury. He tore the pizza from Ayana's hands like a leaf from a calendar and, without a second thought, ripped open the drawer of his captain's desk to withdraw the very item which had provoked the mutiny. Before Ayana's horrified eyes he raised the cat-o'-nine-tails high into the air and brought it down with a vicious swipe, which might have taken Ayana's head off had she not ducked back towards the door.

'Stand fast, mutineer!' bellowed the Captain. He advanced with an almighty stride, as Ayana scrabbled frantically at the door behind her. Stuck! The handle was stuck!

One more stride, and Captain Blight was almost upon her. Up went the lash. Ayana hid her face. Suddenly, however, there was a huge commotion – a cry from the Captain, followed by a hideous crash, then another cry, more distant and higher pitched.

Ayana opened her eyes. The Captain had vanished. Tentatively, Ayana stepped forward, to see, much to her amazement, a gaping hole where the floorboards had been, and down in that hole, the face of her great and loyal friend.

'*That's where the trapdoor goes!*' trilled Petal.

CHAPTER 8

THE REBEL PUPILS, along with Mr Woosnam, gazed in amazement at the prone body of Captain Blight, sprawled across the galley oven.

'He hit his head on a wok,' explained Petal.

'Is he dead?' asked Ayana.

Suki checked his pulse. 'Just stunned,' she replied.

'I do hope you gave him ample chance to show his good side,' said Mr Woosnam.

'Believe me,' said Ayana, 'there wasn't one. Now let's get the dinghy and set him adrift before he wakes up.'

At this point a shrill and fearsome voice resounded down the galley. 'What on *earth* is going on?'

The rebel pupils, and Mr Woosnam, wheeled to face Captain Blight's last loyal ally, Miss Catsnap. Suddenly they stopped being fiery revolutionaries and became quivering infants again, including Mr Woosnam.

'*What* have you done to the Captain?' raged Miss Catsnap.

Ayana took a deep breath and stepped forward. 'There's been a mutiny,' she announced. 'We're in charge now.'

'We're in charge now, *miss,*' corrected Miss Catsnap.

Ayana said nothing.

With her practised teacher's eye, Miss Catsnap looked round for the weakest link. Her gaze fell on Jessica. 'And are you part of this mutiny, Jessica?' she asked.

'Please, miss,' peeped Jessica, 'it's not a mutiny.'

Miss Catsnap positively glowed, having divided the enemy at the first attempt. 'Perhaps you can explain to us what exactly *has* been going on, Jessica,' she declared.

Jessica's lip quivered. Then a tear appeared. 'I want my mum!' she blubbed.

Miss Catsnap looked round the remaining rebels, still gathered about the unconscious figure of Captain Blight. 'I suggest someone gets some smelling salts!' she barked.

Ayana, if she was honest, was still afraid of Miss Catsnap. But she had come too far to turn back now. She drew herself up to her full height which, as we know, was not very high, and looked Miss Catsnap straight in the eye.

'You don't give the orders any more, Miss Catsnap,' she declared. 'I do.'

'Hang on, Ayana,' said Mr Woosnam. 'We haven't agreed that yet.'

'OK,' said Ayana. 'Mr Woosnam does.'

'Or that,' replied Mr Woosnam.

Miss Catsnap turned her attention to her former colleague. She did not look impressed. 'I am senior to Mr Woosnam,' she sniffed.

'Senior to me?' replied Mr Woosnam. 'How is that?'

'I was given charge of the school library,' pronounced Miss Catsnap. 'That put me two points above you on the teachers' salary scale.'

Mr Woosnam looked quite put out. 'Have you forgotten,' he countered, 'that I had responsibility for the Year Six after-school chess club?'

'Fight for it!' yelled Abdi.

'Yeah!' said Ayana. 'And the one who wins gets the boat, and the loser goes in the dinghy with Captain Blight!'

It was one of those moments when a group of junior-school pupils suddenly becomes indistinguishable from a pack of apes. A cry of 'Fight! Fight! Fight!' went up, a cry which got the adrenaline going in the two teachers as well, although Mr Woosnam was still looking less than keen.

'You have to remember,' he said, 'I am opposed to violence.'

'You'll slaughter her, Mr Woosnam!' cried Abdi.

'I shall practise passive resistance, no more,' continued Mr Woosnam.

'Whatever,' said Ayana. Like the others, she could only see one winner in this fight, as Mr Woosnam was at least twice as big as Miss Catsnap.

The cry of 'Fight! Fight! Fight!' went up again, and the two teachers were herded out onto the rain-lashed deck. Under the dim light of a hurricane lamp they faced each other. Miss Catsnap sprang into a stance which suggested she might just have done some martial-arts training. Mr Woosnam, meanwhile, dropped dramatically into a seated position and, in a wavery voice, began to sing 'We Shall Overcome'.

Things were not looking good for Mr Woosnam's supporters.

Miss Catsnap advanced. 'Hi-YA! Hi-YA! Hi-YA!' she cried, executing a series of perfect karate chops.

'Ow! Ow! Ow!' responded Mr Woosnam, followed by another brief burst of 'We Shall Overcome'.

'Do something, Mr Woosnam!' cried Ayana.

'Fight back!' yelled Abdi.

'You're losing!' moaned Iolo Dorito.

'I'm winning the moral victory,' gasped Mr Woosnam. 'Ow!'

There was clearly a lot of history between the two teachers. As Miss Catsnap moved in for the kill, each karate chop was followed by a vengeful cry, such as '*That's* for using my mug and leaving it in the sink!' or '*That's* for jamming the photocopier when I had worksheets to do!'

It must have been one of the most one-sided fights in history. Eventually it was obvious to everybody except Abdi that Miss Catsnap was the winner. Abdi had Mr Woosnam ahead on points, but obviously they had a different points system on Planet Abdi.

There was a grim silence as Miss Catsnap dusted her hands together and Mr Woosnam staggered lamely to his feet.

'I think we have established who is in charge,' declared Miss Catsnap.

The rebel pupils hung their heads, with one exception. Ayana stepped forward with a smug smile, holding her mobile out before her. 'Tough luck, Miss Catsnap,' she declared. 'You've fallen into our trap.'

'Trap?' repeated Miss Catsnap.

'I've got the whole fight on video,' announced Ayana. 'If you don't do as I say, it'll be straight up on YouTube and your teaching career will be over.'

Miss Catsnap's glow of victory suddenly faded. She made a half-hearted attempt to confiscate Ayana's mobile, then realised the game was up. Instead of taking charge of the School Ship Bounty, she found herself in charge of a small rubber dinghy, bobbing like a cork on the great dangerous waves, with only the unconscious Captain for company.

'Set them adrift!' ordered Ayana.

'I do think we should give them something to paddle with,' said Mr Woosnam.

'Then they might come back,' said Ayana.

'It doesn't have to be a good paddle,' commented Mr Woosnam.

The pupils made a quick search of the ship for a suitably rubbish thing to paddle with. Iolo Dorito emerged from the hold, flourishing a rather crudely carved Welsh lovespoon. 'What about this?' he cried.

'That's my lovespoon!' complained Roly Bogart.

The lovespoon looked perfect to Ayana. She was determined that Miss Catsnap be given it. 'If you've got a lovespoon,' she pointed out to Roly, 'someone must be in love with you.'

Ayana's words set off a chorus of 'Roly's got a girlfriend!' which grew and grew in intensity until Roly denied all knowledge of the spoon and insisted it be thrown into the dinghy, taken as far away as possible, never to be seen again.

So it was that a grey-faced Miss Catsnap paddled the dinghy away with her dainty love-spoon oar, slowly, slowly vanishing towards the dark horizon until she and the ghastly Captain could be seen no more.

'I wish I really had videoed that fight,' said Ayana.

CHAPTER 9

THE PUPILS had planned their mutiny well, apart from one small matter – what to do next.

'We can't just stay here,' said Suki. 'As soon as Catsnap gets back to shore, she'll have the authorities on to us.'

'But we don't know how to make the ship go,' complained Iolo.

'Or steer it,' added Roly.

'Or even get the anchor up,' added Jessica.

'Then we'll just have to learn,' said Ayana.

'Fantastic idea!' agreed Mr Woosnam. 'The ship could be a kind of floating educator, and you could all be responsible for drawing up a personal project plan, with attainment targets, and individual merit stickers, and –'

'Suki,' ordered Ayana, 'check out the ship's computer. Abdi – find out how the engine works. Roly – sort out the anchor. Jessica – make tea.'

'Hang on,' said Iolo. 'Who said you were in charge?'

'Suki should be in charge,' said Jessica. 'She got the best marks in this year's tests.'

'What have school tests got to do with this boat?' snapped Ayana. 'School tests are about stupid things like spelling. Spelling isn't going to stop us from sinking.'

'Don't say that!' cried Jessica, tears welling.

'Just hold your horses, Ayana,' said Mr Woosnam. 'We haven't even agreed we need a leader yet.'

'Of course we need a leader!' said Ayana.

'Why?' asked Mr Woosnam.

'To tell people what to do!' replied Ayana.

'Who says we need someone to tell us what to do?' said Mr Woosnam.

'Course we do!' said Ayana. 'Otherwise nothing will get done!'

'I have a different proposal,' announced Mr Woosnam. 'I propose that we all sit down together and discuss things, then make decisions which everybody is happy with. You know, a bit like School Council, except when we decide something, it actually happens.'

'Eh?' said Ayana. 'We'll never agree!'

'We could have votes,' suggested Suki.

'That's a very good suggestion, Suki,' replied Mr Woosnam. 'Except, if we have votes, some people will end up being unhappy with the decision. It's much better if we keep discussing till everybody agrees.'

'What if we don't ever agree?' said Ayana.

'We have to make compromises,' replied Mr Woosnam.

At this point a huge wave hit the SS Bounty and a great wall of seawater showered the mutineers.

'I want to go home!' cried Jessica.

'We're not going home!' cried Ayana.

'How will we ever agree?' cried Suki, despairingly.

'As I said,' explained Mr Woosnam. 'We have to make compromises. For example, if Jessica wants us to go home, and Ayana doesn't, we could agree to go halfway home.'

'That's mad!' cried Jessica.

'That's mental!' cried Ayana.

'See?' said Mr Woosnam. 'You're agreeing already.'

The discussion was beginning to resemble one of Mr Woosnam's lessons, and if there had been windows, people would have been gazing out of them.

'Why don't we just have an election to elect who's leader?' suggested Petal.

There were murmurs of agreement.

'I thought we'd just decided not to have a leader,' said Mr Woosnam.

'No we didn't,' said Ayana. 'That was just what you said.'

'Let's have a vote on it,' said Abdi.

'But we haven't agreed to have votes,' countered Mr Woosnam.

Another massive wave hit the boat.

'I vote we elect a leader,' said Abdi, raising his hand.

Ayana, Petal, Suki and Roly also raised their hands. Despite Mr Woosnam's protests they declared the vote won.

Ayana proposed herself as leader. No one else wanted to stand. Ayana was duly elected.

'I know,' said Suki. 'Why don't we do what the old Celtic tribes did, and elect an heir as well, so if the first leader dies, or annoys us, we replace them?'

'I'm not going to die!' said Ayana.

'You might annoy us,' said Abdi.

'I propose Suki as heir,' said Petal.

Ayana shot Petal a dark look which Petal didn't really understand. But the idea of Suki as heir was a popular one, and despite the fact she claimed she didn't want the job, she was duly elected.

'Right,' said Ayana. 'Suki – check out the ship's computer. Abdi – find out how the engine works. Roly – sort out the anchor. Jessica – make tea.'

There was a small grumble of protest from Jessica, and a louder one from Mr Woosnam. 'I'm really not happy with this,' he mumbled.

Ayana's reign as leader/captain/queen of the SS Bounty got off to a flying start. Searching through the Captain's desk, she came across a tattered old pamphlet which, she soon realised, was worth its weight in gold. She called everyone together to parade her find.

'Fantastic news!' she declared. 'I've found the Owner's Manual for the SS Bounty. There's even a guarantee with it, so if anything breaks, we can get it fixed.'

'How long does the guarantee last?' asked Petal.

'Six months,' replied Ayana.

'What's the date on it?' asked Suki.

'1951,' replied Ayana.

'Never mind,' said Mr Woosnam. 'Does it tell us how to weigh anchor, because Roly and I are having a hell of a job pulling it up.'

'Here it is,' replied Ayana. 'Page eleven.'

'What about starting the engine?' asked Abdi. 'It's nothing like my brother's moped.'

'Page five,' replied Ayana.

'Maybe we could photocopy the pages and make some laminated worksheets from them,' suggested Mr Woosnam.

Ayana held the pamphlet to her chest. 'I'm keeping it on the bridge,' she declared. 'If anyone wants to know anything, they can ask me.'

Knowing looks were exchanged between Suki and Mr Woosnam. For the moment, though, everyone went along with Ayana, which meant there was a constant queue at her door. Eventually, however, everyone had learnt what they had to learn: the engine was started, the anchor was weighed, and for the first time in yonks, or even longer, the SS Bounty began to plough through the waves.

This only left the small matter of which way to go.

Luckily, Suki was at work on the ship's computer, an ancient old thing which took up half the space on the bridge. She had found a program which showed how to set a ship's course, and was studying a drop-down menu labelled DESTINATIONS.

'If we just keep heading away from Wales,' she said, 'we should come to Ireland.'

'Hmm,' said Ayana. 'I was thinking about America.'

Ayana hadn't really been thinking about America. She just preferred to disagree with Suki.

'But we haven't got enough fuel to get to America,' argued Suki.

'Then we'll refuel on the way,' suggested Ayana.

'Where?' asked Suki.

Ayana glanced at the globe which sat on her captain's desk, and traced a finger from Wales in the direction of the big country across the ocean. 'What about here?' she suggested, finding an island on the way.

Suki checked the blob of land under Ayana's finger. 'That's Ireland,' she pointed out.

'OK,' said Ayana. 'We'll go there.'

With a sigh, Suki clicked on the drop-down menu, checked the co-ordinates, and set the ship's course. Having done that, she thought it might be an idea to check the local news, just in case there was any mention of the fact that seven pupils and a teacher had taken over a boat and sent the Captain home in a rubber dinghy.

To her dismay, Suki found the following on www.whatsupcymru.com:

MUTINY ON THE SCHOOL SHIP BOUNTY
Captain Blight Vows Revenge

Captain and head teacher Horatio Blight, MBE, swore an oath of revenge last night after his vessel, the SS Bounty, had been taken over by a mob of schoolchildren. Blight, 57, said, 'No matter how long it takes or what desperate measures I am driven to, I shall have that vessel back under my control and the criminal rabble brought to justice.'

The experienced and much-respected sailor is believed to have chartered a motor boat in order to give chase to the rogue ship, which is no longer at anchor off Abertwit. The children were originally pupils of Owen Glyn Bowen Primary, before the school fell down a hole.

'I knew we shouldn't have given them that lovespoon,' said Ayana, when Suki showed her the news story.'

'We'd better get down the engine room and see if they can get any more speed,' said Suki.

'Shh,' said Ayana. 'I'm thinking.'

Ayana thought. 'We'd better get down the engine room and see if they can get any more speed,' she said.

Suki bit her lip and said nothing.

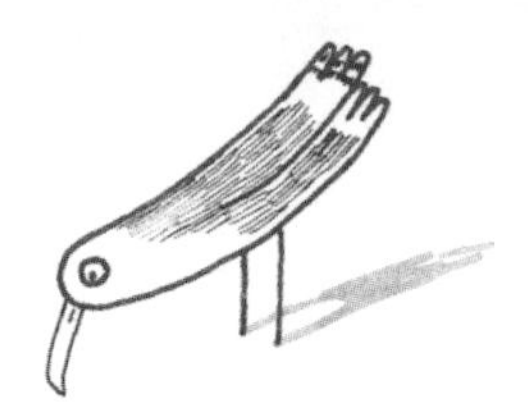

CHAPTER 10

THE THREAT OF Captain Blight worked wonders on the shipmates of SS Bounty. Never had they been so keen to learn. Without a laminated worksheet in sight, Abdi and Roly became experts on the engine, Petal learned how to steer, Iolo mastered the electrics and Suki sussed out not only the computer but the radar and the sonar. Mr Woosnam didn't learn much but was happy to serve as a general dogsbody, while Jessica not only made endless urns of tea but also an attractive appliqué ship's flag. There had been a big debate over what should be on this flag, but to Mr Woosnam's delight the pupils reached a happy compromise, as a result of which the Welsh dragon and crossbones flew proudly from the SS Bounty's stern.

Despite the fact the ship kept up a good speed, however, no land was coming into sight, and as time dragged on, a new problem surfaced.

'The food supplies are running out,' declared Jessica. 'All we've got is one can of spaghetti and twenty-five tins of laver bread.'

'Laver bread?' moaned Iolo. 'That tastes like seaweed!'

'It is seaweed, stupid,' said Abdi.

'I've got some alfalfa seeds in my bag,' said Mr Woosnam. 'If we put them on wet cotton wool, we could have alfalfa sprouts in three days' time.'

'A ship's crew can't live on alfalfa sprouts!' cried Ayana.

'They're very nutritious,' protested Mr Woosnam.

'They taste even worse than laver bread,' moaned Iolo.

'What do you propose we do, Ayana?' asked Suki. There was a hint of challenge in her voice.

'What do *you* propose?' countered Ayana.

'I'm not the captain,' replied Suki. 'It's not my job to make decisions.'

Ayana did her best not to show she was rattled. 'OK,' she said. 'This is what we've got to do.'

Everyone was all ears.

'We've got to kill something,' declared Ayana.

There was a gasp from Jessica and a little 'oh no' from Mr Woosnam.

'The sea's full of fish,' continued Ayana. 'We've just got to catch some of them.'

'Actually,' said Mr Woosnam, 'stocks of fish are steadily dwindling due to overfishing, and many species, for example cod, are under grave threat.'

'So are we,' replied Ayana.

'I know,' said Iolo. 'We could tie all the hammocks together, and make a net.'

'That's a very intelligent idea, Iolo,' said Mr Woosnam, 'but we can't do it.'

'Why not?' complained Iolo.

'Nets are very bad,' replied Mr Woosnam. 'Dolphins can get caught in them.'

'So?' said Ayana. 'We could eat the dolphins.'

Mr Woosnam's jaw dropped. 'Eat a dolphin?' he gasped. 'Dolphins are the most intelligent creatures in the sea! Some believe their intelligence is second only to humans. They arc mammals, just like us, they show signs of distress when their mate is injured, and some scientists believe they have feelings similar to human emotions.'

Ayana nodded thoughtfully. 'Having said that,' she said, 'there must be loads of meat on them.'

'We are not eating a dolphin and that's final,' replied Mr Woosnam.

'I thought you said we should make all the decisions together,' said Ayana.

Mr Woosnam looked uncomfortable. 'Is anyone really in favour of eating a dolphin?' he asked.

Ayana raised her hand.

'You're just being silly,' said Mr Woosnam.

'No I'm not,' said Ayana. 'I'd rather eat a dolphin than starve.'

'Well, you're outvoted,' said Mr Woosnam.

'No, we can't have votes, you said!' replied Ayana. 'We've got to keep debating till we reach a compromise.'

'Ayana wants to kill a dolphin,' said Suki. 'Mr Woosnam says we mustn't. How can we reach a compromise about that?'

'Maybe we could just wound a dolphin,' suggested Petal.

Suki scowled. 'What would be the point of that?' she scoffed.

Petal thought for a moment. 'Like, if you wanted to eat a cow, but you didn't want to kill it, you could just cut one of its legs off.'

'Petal!' said Suki. 'That is absurd.'

'No it isn't!' snapped Ayana. 'You could eat the leg and the cow could carry on living with a false one, so nerr!'

'I see,' replied Mr Woosnam, 'and what part of a dolphin do you think we could cut off?'

Ayana thought for a moment. 'The fin?' she suggested.

'It needs its fin to steer with,' replied Mr Woosnam.

'I don't know!' snapped Ayana. 'Ask the dolphin!'

'You see,' said Suki. 'It's a stupid idea.'

'At least I have ideas,' replied Ayana.

'Look,' said Mr Woosnam, 'we do have to eat, so how about if we try to catch fish, but by traditional methods, such as a rod and line?'

'But we haven't got rods and lines,' protested Iolo.

'Then we'll have a handicrafts lesson, and make them!' declared Mr Woosnam, brimming with excitement at such a thought.

CHAPTER 11

THE HANDICRAFTS LESSON was a great success. Everybody managed to find a stick. Jessica found some twine in her sewing box, and also some hooks which the pupils sharpened by rubbing them between fifty pence pieces. Eventually everyone had a rod and line which was perfect for catching fish, apart from one small problem.

'What are we going to use for bait?' asked Roly.

'We need worms,' declared Suki.

'Iolo has got worms!' blurted Abdi.

'I have not!' protested Iolo.

'Yes you have!' cried Abdi. 'We heard the nurse telling Mrs Mostyn!'

'That was a joke!' complained Iolo. 'She said I was always eating, so I must have worms!'

'What, earthworms?' asked Petal, who, as usual, was a bit slow on the uptake.

'Let's not go into this,' suggested Mr Woosnam.

'I know,' said Ayana. 'What if we use the can of spaghetti, and make it look like worms?'

'That's the last can!' moaned Iolo.

'So?' replied Ayana. 'We'll get two strands each out of that – but if we use it as bait, we'll have two fish each!'

There were murmurs of opposition, but Ayana reminded everybody (in case they had forgotten) that she was captain, and the plan was put into effect. The pupils lined up on either side of the ship, equipped with their handmade rods and fake worms, and the fish hunt began.

It was a not a notable success.

In fact, they caught nothing.

'Can't you stop the boat rocking, Ayana?' asked Petal.

'If you can stop the sea rocking,' replied Ayana.

'We're never going to catch anything!' moaned Iolo.

'But at least we're trying,' said Mr Woosnam, consolingly, except it didn't console anybody.

Hours passed. Abdi, who hated sitting still for anything, declared he'd got a different plan, and disappeared. Iolo and Petal had an argument about whether they should have eaten the spaghetti. Mr Woosnam offered to sing some old Suzanne Vega songs, but everyone suddenly became concerned about his health and the need to save his energy.

Then, just as everyone was about to give up, there was a cry from the rear of the boat: 'I've got one!'

Abdi scuttled back into view, holding a fist aloft.

'At last!' cried Ayana.

'Is it a big one?' asked Iolo.

'Whopping!' cried Abdi.

Mr Woosnam looked concerned. 'It's not . . . a dolphin, is it, Abdi?' he asked.

'Nah,' said Abdi. 'I think it's a tuna.'

'I love tuna!' said Roly.

'Did it fight?' asked Iolo.

'No,' said Abdi. 'It just kind of . . . keeled over.'

'Was it easy to pull in?' asked Suki.

'I never caught it like that,' replied Abdi.

Mr Woosnam's suspicious frown returned. 'How *did* you catch it, Abdi?' he asked.

'With my arrows,' replied Abdi. He proudly displayed the remains of a set of championship darts.

'You killed it with a *dart*?' said Ayana.

'Bullseye!' said Abdi, grinning widely.

'So . . . where is it?' asked Suki.

'Follow me,' said Abdi.

He led the hungry crowd to the starboard side of the ship. Then he pointed to a spot in the sea about two hundred metres behind them. 'It's about there,' he declared.

Ayana's face dropped. 'It's still in the sea?' she exclaimed.

'Yeah,' said Abdi. 'We've just got to turn round and get it.'

'Abdi,' replied Ayana. 'We are not turning this ship around to look for one stupid dead fish.'

'The sharks have probably had it anyway,' moaned Iolo.

'Are there sharks?' gasped Jessica.

'Calm down, Jessica,' said Mr Woosnam. 'There's nothing dangerous in these waters.'

'Correction,' said Ayana. 'There is one thing that's dangerous, and he's called Captain Blight, and he is the reason I'm not turning this ship around to look for a dead fish!'

Suki laid a consoling hand on Abdi's shoulder. 'Well done anyway, Abdi,' she said. 'At least you tried.'

'I was going to say that,' blurted Ayana.

Suki turned to the other pupils. 'It looks like we've wasted our last tin of spaghetti,' she declared.

There were murmurs of agreement.

'Anyone for laver bread?' twittered Jessica.

CHAPTER 12

ANOTHER DAY PASSED. Still no land came into view.

'Are you sure we're going the right way?' Ayana asked Suki. 'Ireland takes two hours on the Holyhead ferry.'

'The Holyhead ferry is faster,' replied Suki.

'Yeah, but even so,' said Ayana. 'We've been going two and a half days!'

'The computer set the course,' replied Suki. 'Argue with the computer.'

It all seemed suspicious to Ayana. Was Suki deliberately keeping them at sea to provoke a mutiny? No one would stand eating laver bread for tea again.

Then Ayana had an idea. She sent for Roly Bogart and swore him to secrecy.

'I am going to lend you something very precious of mine,' she said.

So saying, Ayana opened her bag and took out a home-made weapon of most wondrous beauty.

'Wow,' said Roly. 'A catapult!'

'You must guard it with your life,' warned Ayana.

'What am I going to do with it?' asked Roly.

'You may have noticed,' said Ayana, 'a lot of birds have been following the ship.'

'I've got to kill one?' gasped Roly.

'I prefer the word "dispatch",' declared Ayana.

'I don't think I could ki- . . . dispatch a bird,' said Roly.

'You'll be a hero, Roly!' hissed Ayana.

Roly weakened.

'Or would you prefer Captain Blight to catch us,' added Ayana, 'and end up . . . like the *mutineer*?'

Roly gave a weak cry as the memory of the terrible incident with the skeleton came back to him.

'Don't let Woosnam see you,' said Ayana, pressing the catapult into his quivering hand.

For an hour or so there was no further sign of Roly. Then came an excited cry. 'I've got one!'

All the crew gathered on deck as Roly danced towards them, waving his catapult. 'Dropped like a stone!' he cried.

'Dropped?' queried Mr Woosnam. 'How can a fish drop?'

'Not a fish!' cried Roly. 'A bird!'

'You've killed a bird?' said Petal, a look of deep concern on her face.

'It's massive!' cried Roly. 'The biggest bird I've ever seen! I let fly and WHAM! Bullseye! Hit the deck.'

By now all the pupils had gathered. 'OK, Roly,' said Ayana. 'Where is it?'

'Right by the bows,' replied Roly. 'I think it's a gull,' he added.

Half-excited, half-appalled, the posse of pupils followed Roly to the front of the ship. There on the deck, stone still, wings outstretched, was the most humungous seabird any of them had ever seen.

Mr Woosnam's face fell. 'Roly,' he said. 'That's not a gull. That's an albatross.'

'Tidy!' said Roly.

'Roly,' explained Mr Woosnam, 'the albatross is known as the sailor's friend. To kill one is just about the worst thing a sailor can do.'

NOTE FROM PURRPANTS

There's probably some smarty-pants out there who knows that the albatross is actually a bird of the southern oceans, which, as we know, is not where the SS Bounty is sailing. Well nerr, because albatrosses have been sighted in the north, and have even tried to breed in Scotland, which is not all that far from Wales. To be honest, they were probably very stupid albatrosses, hopelessly lost, but then it would have to be a pretty dim albatross to let Roly Bogart shoot it.

'Wh-what will happen, Mr Woosnam?' asked Jessica.

'Probably nothing, Jessica,' replied Mr Woosnam, unconvincingly.

'It brings bad luck, doesn't it, sir?' said Abdi.

'That's just a silly old superstition,' replied Mr Woosnam.

'I knew it,' said Abdi.

'We're all going to die,' said Iolo.

Jessica began to cry. The others looked at the giant bird with new eyes. Now it was a sinister thing, a thing of great portent, a huge and inescapable omen of doom.

'Who gave Roly the catapult?' asked Mr Woosnam.

All eyes fell on Ayana.

'Please, sir,' said Roly, 'Ayana said we can't catch fish so we should shoot at birds.'

'It was meant as a – a game,' gabbled Ayana.

'A game?' replied Suki. 'What kind of game?'

'Like chicken,' cried Ayana. 'You know, where you race across the road when cars are coming.'

'Exactly,' said Mr Woosnam. 'An extremely stupid game.'

'Anyway,' blurted Ayana, 'it might not be dead.'

'Of course it's dead!' scoffed Suki.

'I saw its eye move!' said Ayana.

'No you didn't,' replied Suki.

'Yes I did!' insisted Ayana. 'It's just stunned!'

'What are you going to do?' scoffed Iolo. 'Give it the kiss of life?'

'Good idea,' said Ayana. 'I'll take it up to the bridge and give it mouth-to-beak sussitation.'

'Resuscitation,' corrected Mr Woosnam.

'That too,' said Ayana.

CHAPTER 13

Ayana and Petal gazed at the great bird at their feet and willed it to twitch.

'Are you really going to give it the kiss of life?' asked Petal.

'No way!' said Ayana. 'Would you kiss a bird?'

'A robin maybe,' replied Petal.

'A robin hasn't got a stonking great beak that smells of fish,' said Ayana.

'If we knew what its favourite music was, we could play that,' suggested Petal. 'That's how they bring people out of comas.'

'Maybe we could get its favourite pop star to make a bedside visit,' sneered Ayana.

'That's an idea,' said Petal, who had never really got to grips with sarcasm.

Ayana thought for a while. Then an idea occurred. 'Hmm,' she mused. 'We haven't *got* to bring it back to life. All that matters is that people *believe* it's alive.'

'Eh?' said Petal. 'How will we do that?'

'Have you got any black clothes?'

'I've got some black leggings,' replied Petal, 'and a black top. Why?'

'Put them on tomorrow morning,' said Ayana, 'just before dawn, while everyone's asleep. Then come up here.'

Ayana would say nothing more about her plan, which worried Petal, but as usual Petal had great faith in her best friend, and very early next morning duly arrived on the bridge dressed from head to toe in black.

'Excellent,' said Ayana. 'Now we just have to strap the albatross to your back.'

'Excuse me?' said Petal.

Ayana repeated herself, as Petal was obviously hard of hearing.

'Strap the albatross to my back?' gasped Petal. 'Why on earth are you going to do that?'

'It's very simple,' replied Ayana. 'Now it's dark, you go out on deck, keep low to the ground, and start running around flapping your arms. If I can catch it right on my mobile, it'll look like the albatross is moving by itself.'

Petal tried to take this in. She'd been involved in some mental schemes with Ayana, but nothing like this. 'I can't do it,' she declared.

'Course you can do it!' said Ayana. 'It's in your blood!'

'Why is it in my blood?' asked Petal.

'Your mum had detox in her face,' replied Ayana.

'Detox?' repeated Petal, baffled.

'You know,' said Ayana, 'the stuff that made her eyes look startled.'

'Botox?' suggested Petal.

'Botox,' repeated Ayana. 'That's the one.'

Petal was bewildered. 'Having botox put in your face,' she declared, 'is nothing like having an albatross strapped to your back.'

'Course it is!' claimed Ayana. 'It's a rock star thing! You know, like biting the head off a live bat.'

'Have I got to do that as well?' gasped Petal.

'Just relax, Petal,' replied Ayana. 'All I'm going to do is use these bungees to fix the albatross's wings to your arms. Then the rest should just hang over you. You'll have to keep your head still, mind, so the albatross's head stays on top and doesn't flop to one side.'

If truth be told, Petal still wasn't happy about the plan. It seemed to her so much simpler just to admit the bird was dead, but Ayana was having none of that. Soon Petal was trussed up in the weirdest fancy-dress costume she'd ever worn, and the heaviest at that. It really was a big bird, especially when it was on your back with its wings tied to your arms.

'Once around the deck should do,' said Ayana.

Ayana slowed the ship and tied the wheel, then guided Petal out of the bridge and down the steps. It wasn't at all comfortable for Ayana's loyal mate.

'When I say "action", run round madly, flapping your arms,' ordered Ayana.

Petal prepared herself.

'Action!'

With great difficulty, Petal set off round the deck in a peculiar crouching waddle, flapping her arms as best she could, while Ayana caught the whole tortured business on her mobile. The albatross did indeed look like it was flying, but more like a clown plane from a circus act than a graceful, soaring seabird.

Just as Petal completed her first lap, something bizarre occurred. An unearthly cry filled the air, loud enough to wake the dead.

'Petal!' hissed Ayana. 'You don't have to make the noises!'

Petal stopped. 'Wasn't that you?' she asked.

'Of course it wasn't me!' hissed Ayana.

'It wasn't me either,' replied Petal.

'Then who was it?' asked Ayana.

Slowly, fearfully, Petal's eyes roved upwards. As they did so, the albatross's great beak opened and another fearsome cry filled the air.

'It *is* alive!' screamed Petal.

Hardly had the words escaped her lips than the albatross began to struggle with all the strength in its body. Suddenly it was Petal's arms which were being beaten up and down, by a mighty force which almost dragged her off her feet.

'Help! Help!' she yelled.

'Shh!' cried Ayana.

It was too late. The whole ship was awoken, and bleary-eyed shipmates were already arriving on deck to witness a spectacle more bizarre than any of their dreams. By now the albatross's screeches could surely be heard back in Abertwit, while Petal's screams almost matched them. Somehow one of the great bird's wings had got loose and was flapping like a sheet in a gale, so hard that it looked as if the albatross might take off with Petal still attached.

'What on *earth* is going on?' cried Mr Woosnam.

'It's all planned!' cried Ayana. She ploughed into the middle of the frenzy, and with some difficulty got the bungees off Petal's other arm. The albatross flopped to the ground, then staggered to its feet, took a few steps, and was shakily airborne. The whole crowd watched in amazement as it flew unsteadily into the distance.

'There you go,' said Ayana. 'It's alive.'

Mr Woosnam viewed her with disbelief. 'You tied the albatross to Petal!' he blurted.

'She wanted to do it!' protested Ayana.

'You might have killed her,' declared Suki.

'You're fine, aren't you, Petal?' said Ayana, laying a consoling hand on her best friend's arm, but getting only desperate pants of breath for reply.

Mr Woosnam's face became deadly serious. 'I think we've reached the end of the line, Ayana,' he declared.

'How do you mean?' asked Ayana.

'For you as captain,' replied Mr Woosnam.

'That's not for you to decide,' said Ayana.

'Very well,' replied Mr Woosnam. 'Who thinks Suki should take over as captain?' he asked.

A couple of uncertain arms were raised. More sheepishly followed.

‘This,’ declared Ayana, ‘is mutiny.’

‘No it isn’t,’ replied Mr Woosnam. ‘It’s democracy.’

Ayana looked round for support. Even Petal looked away.

‘Don’t listen to Woosnam!’ cried Ayana. ‘He’s a teacher! He just can’t take someone else giving the orders!’

‘Oh, really,’ replied Mr Woosnam.

‘Look at the way he lost that fight,’ said Ayana. ‘It was like he wanted to get sent away with Captain Blight. And when he didn’t, he just stayed here to spy on us!’

‘That’s ridiculous,’ said Mr Woosnam.

‘How do we know he isn’t sending secret messages to Captain Blight?’ rasped Ayana.

‘Don’t waste your breath, Ayana,’ said Suki. ‘No one’s listening.’

‘Teacher’s pet!’ scoffed Ayana.

‘That’s no way to talk to your captain,’ replied Suki.

‘You’re not captain!’ cried Ayana.

‘Am,’ said Suki.

‘Are not,’ said Ayana.

‘Am,’ said Suki.

‘Fight you for it,’ said Ayana.

As soon as Ayana said this she realised she’d made a serious mistake. Suki was, after all, a junior black belt in tae kwon do. But before Ayana could think of a way out, the cry of 'fight, fight!' went up, drowning the half-hearted protests of Mr Woosnam. A space was cleared on the deck and Ayana found herself face to face with a deadly serious enemy.

'After three,' said Iolo, who'd elected himself referee.

'One . . .'

'Two . . .'

'Land!' cried Abdi. 'Land ahoy!'

In a millisecond the fight was forgotten in a mad scramble to the port side where Abdi was standing. Sure enough, a shoreline was clearly visible, and drawing closer by the second. But there were no signs of houses, or parks, or even trees. The land that approached looked like something off the moon, with great flat wastes of black rock and, in the distance, misty snow-topped mountains.

'I don't remember Ireland looking like this,' said Petal.

'It must be Ireland,' said Suki. 'That's where I set the course for.' She took out her mobile, brought up the net and logged in to the ship's guidance program. Then her face dropped. 'Oh dear,' she said.

'What's the problem, Suki?' asked Mr Woosnam.

'I – I must have clicked the next word up,' gabbled Suki.

'So this isn't Ireland?' asked Iolo.

'No,' replied Suki. 'It's Iceland.'

A quiet smile of satisfaction spread over Ayana's face as howls of outrage echoed around the ship. So that's why it had taken so long! So that's why they were all starving! And to make matters worse, they couldn't turn back, because Captain Blight was on their tail!

Speaking of which . . .

'What's that boat?' cried Abdi.

Fearfully, everyone followed Abdi's pointing finger. Sure enough, there was a big boat not far ahead, the like of which they'd never seen before. At the bows was some kind of weapon, a gun maybe, and at the stern a pair of giant metal jaws poking up into the early morning sky. The side of the boat was stained red, as if a god had accidentally emptied a pot of paint over it.

Then something else came into view. Something dark, sleek, rising out of the water and then back down again.

'A whale!' cried Ayana. Ayana had rooted for whales ever since Captain Blight had described his whaling adventures. She and the shipmates watched in wonder as two, three, four more of the great beasts broke the surface, shining black in the morning sun.

'Quick! Let's take pictures!' cried Abdi, but as the shipmates reached for their mobiles, Ayana noticed something which made her blood run cold. A posse of men had appeared at the bows of the big boat, and were aiming the weapon straight at the school of whales.

'They're going to kill them!' she cried.

The delight of the shipmates turned to horror. But at that second, something else came into view. It was a motorised rubber dinghy, with three people on board, speeding directly between the harpoon and the whales. Two of the people held up a banner while the other pulled out a video camera and started filming the men on the big boat.

'Sea Angels!' cried Mr Woosnam.

Everyone cheered. They'd all heard of the brave whale defenders, but no one had imagined seeing them in action.

The men with the harpoon did not look so pleased. There were angry cries, and fierce gestures, but the people in the Sea Angels' dinghy held their nerve. Suddenly, however, a violent jet of water spewed out from the side of the whaleboat. One of the people holding the banner was knocked clean out of the dinghy. The others turned to save him, and as they did so were also caught full force. The dinghy was capsized and all three Sea Angels thrashed helplessly in the water.

The shipmates of the SS Bounty were stunned silent. But while everyone else felt hopeless and helpless, Ayana's eyes smouldered with righteous energy. The voices of her ancestors rose inside her in a mighty chorus. Suddenly she burst into life.

'Roly!' she cried. 'Get the rope ladder! Abdi, Woosie – the lifesavers! Petal – take the wheel, full steam ahead! Jessica – make me a cardboard funnel, a big one! Iolo, Suki – get your mobiles out and video everything!'

Inspired by Ayana's passion, the shipmates exploded into action. Before the astonished eyes of the whalers, the SS Bounty forged into the space between the whaler and the whales, its deck alive with manic schoolkids. Soon the grateful Sea Angels were clinging onto life-savers and splashing their way to the SS Bounty's rope ladder, while Ayana was perched on the ship's rails with a cardboard funnel pressed to her lips.

'Stand clear of the harpoon!' she cried. 'Put down the water jet! We are International

WhaleSave and we are videoing your every move!'

The whalers looked from Ayana to Iolo and Suki, then to the dragon and crossbones fluttering in the breeze. International WhaleSave? What kind of organisation could this possibly be? But the thought of firing a water cannon at a bunch of kids, and the whole world seeing it on the TV news . . . that made even the hardest head on the whaleboat think twice.

For a minute or so there was stalemate. Then the tannoy on the whaleboat burst into life.

'Move away from the area!' a voice blared. 'This ship is operating within the law and you have no right to interfere with our lawful business!'

'Is that true, Mr Woosnam?' asked Abdi.

'Um . . .' said Mr Woosnam. 'I'm not quite sure.'

NOTE FROM PURRPANTS

There's probably some clever clogs out there who knows that Iceland banned whaling for whale-meat in August 2008. Ah, but did you know that some whales can still be slaughtered for 'scientific research'? Or that Iceland's neighbour Norway still hunts whales? There, you're not as clever as you thought you were, so stop trying to mess up this story.

'This is your final warning!' barked the tannoy. 'Move away from the area.'

'We'd better do as they say,' murmured Mr Woosnam.

Ayana didn't seem to hear. The voice from the whaler reminded her of Captain Blight, and the fire in her eyes burned brighter than ever.

'We don't care about the law!' she boomed. 'We care about the whales!'

Inspired by Ayana's defiance, her shipmates raised their fists and cheered, all except Suki and Iolo, but that was only because they were videoing the whalers' every move.

'Where is your teacher?' demanded the voice on the tannoy.

Mr Woosnam ducked down behind the ship's lifeboat. Ayana once more raised the funnel to her lips.

'We have no teacher!' she cried. 'We are mutineers!'

There was another cheer from Ayana's

shipmates, even Jessica. Suddenly it was not scary to be a mutineer any more – it was great.

For several more minutes the stand-off continued. The whalers with the water cannon argued with each other. The whalers with the harpoon were still and silent. Then, with no announcement, the whaleboat began to steam away. Away from the SS Bounty, and away from the whales. As it grew smaller and smaller, it was clear it had retreated from the conflict for good. Ayana and her shipmates had won. The whales would live to see another day.

'Three cheers for Ayana!' cried Abdi.

More cheers echoed round the SS Bounty, not least from the three Sea Angels. In all the excitement the shipmates had barely paid any attention to the newcomers. Now they turned their eyes to the three figures they'd saved, two of whom had beards, while the third was clean-shaven, or rather not shaven at all, seeing as she was a woman. She introduced herself as Gisela, and her friends as Jordi and Paolo. They were fascinated to know all about the SS Bounty, and nodded with approval as Ayana told the story of how they'd made the old whaling captain walk the plank, then set off for Iceland to save the whales.

'We must treat you to breakfast,' said Gisela.

That got the loudest cheer of all.

CHAPTER 14

IT WAS THE best breakfast the shipmates had ever had, with rye bread and scrambled egg, ocean shrimps and smoked salmon, cinnamon rolls and choux buns, all washed down with hot coffee and fresh juice. Afterwards they all went to a warm, milky lagoon in the lava fields and sat in steamy luxury, reflecting back over their amazing adventure.

'I wish life could always be like this,' mused Petal.

'Actually,' said Gisela, 'there's something we want to propose to you.'

The shipmates were all ears.

'The Sea Angels have been left a large sum of money,' Gisela continued, 'and we have been asked to set up an Educational Foundation.'

The shipmates nodded eagerly, even though they had no idea what an Educational Foundation was.

'We weren't sure how to go about this,' said Gisela, 'but you have given us a great idea.'

The shipmates glowed with self-satisfaction.

'Our proposal,' continued Gisela, 'is that the SS Bounty sails the oceans of the world, helping to stop the terrible things which threaten our planet, and sending out news stories which all the children of the world will want to read.'

'Cool!' cried Iolo.

'Wicked!' cried Abdi.

'When will I get to see Mummy?' whimpered Jessica.

'Have no fears,' replied Gisela. 'That will all be sorted for you.'

Ayana narrowed her eyes suspiciously. 'Will we still have to do projects?' she asked.

'*This* is your project,' replied Gisela. 'Everything will be entirely up to you – with a little helpful advice from us.'

Ayana smiled broadly, and her ancestors, had they been around, would surely have smiled too.

'Is it a deal?' asked Gisela.

'Deal!' cried the shipmates, as one. With that, Abdi splashed Iolo, Iolo splashed Petal, and soon a full-on water-fight was in progress, the excited cries from which could be surely heard as far as the SS Bounty as it lay at anchor in the bay. What adventures lay ahead of that ship now!

EPURRLOGUE - note from Purrpants

Yes, the future looked rosy for Ayana and the mutineers, apart from one small cloud on the horizon - or to be more precise, one small boat, with a familiar grim figure at the wheel, focussing remorselessly on the enemy he would never forget.